Robert Harries Jones

The Japhetic Races

Robert Harries Jones

The Japhetic Races

Reprint of the original, first published in 1857.

1st Edition 2023 | ISBN: 978-3-37517-124-7

Salzwasser Verlag is an imprint of Outlook Verlagsgesellschaft mbH.

Verlag (Publisher): Outlook Verlag GmbH, Zeilweg 44, 60439 Frankfurt, Deutschland
Vertretungsberechtigt (Authorized to represent): E. Roepke, Zeilweg 44, 60439 Frankfurt, Deutschland
Druck (Print): Books on Demand GmbH, In de Tarpen 42, 22848 Norderstedt, Deutschland

THE JAPHETIC RACES.

A

HISTORICAL AND ETHNOLOGICAL INQUIRY

INTO THE

CONSANGUINITY

OF

VARIOUS EUROPEAN RACES.

AN INAUGURAL-DISSERTATION

UPON OBTAINING THE DEGREE OF

DOCTOR OF PHILOSOPHY

IN THE

UNIVERSITY OF GÖTTINGEN

BY THE REVEREND

R. HARRIES JONES

SENIOR CURATE AND SUB-LECTURER OF THE PARISH CHURCH
BOLTON LE MOORS.

GÖTTINGEN:

PRINTED AT THE UNIVERSITY PRESS BY W. FR. KAESTNER.

1857.

PART THE FIRST.

The subject of the present essay, is the original relationship of the Japhetic Nations of Europe and Asia; and it will embrace an investigation, and contain a confirmation of the genealogical Table as given by Moses in the tenth chapter of Genesis, and also an attempt to shew from profane records, both Grecian and Roman Historians, how the present nations especially of Europe migrated from their original home, and where, according to the same authorities, that original home was most likely, if not positively located. The investigation', then, rests principally upon the testimony of heathen authors; but during the last thirty or forty years an important auxiliary has been developed in the philological investigations.

It is necessary when we start tracing ancient nations and ancient names, to prepare our minds for some latitude in the different manner of spelling used by different authors, at different and the same era; and to expect, also, that cognate letters should often be interchanged in the same names, and others somewhat,

and apparently arbitrarily, interchanged, to snit the genius of the native language of those who used the
words. But snch changes as these are only what are
continually occurring, and from minute observation and
careful comparison, they have been reduced almost into
a perfect system; so that any one who has devoted his
attention to languages, can instantly and distinctly pronounce whether snch and snch change was or was not
likely ever to have occurred.

The English word *eye* is in French *oeil*, — you see
there is an *l* inserted which is preserved or retained from
the Latin *oculus;* but in Italian it is *occhio*, with the *l*
dropped; in Spanish *ajo,* in German *auge*, in Hebrew
עַיִן and in Welsh llygaid, with a donble *ll* prefixed,
which is not at all an nnsual thing; for we have the
English *even* and German *eben* reprodnced, or, in a
more primitive form, in Welsh *llyfu;* the English *flow* in
the Welsh *llifo*, *load* in the Welsh llwyth, and so with
many other words of a similar philology.

The English word *bear* is of the same sort as the
Latin *fero* and pario, that again is of the same sort
as the Greek word φέρω, and that is cleary the same
word as the Hebrew פָּרָה, and that again is the same
as the Sanscrit *bhri*, Gothic *bairan*, German gebären; all
meaning precisely the same thing, and all retaining the
same ancient stamina, althongh modified and altered by
the different nations among whom the word is found.

The English word *wine* is the latin *vinum*, French
vin, Italian *vino*, Greek οἶνος, Hebrew יַיִן, Armenian

gini and Welsh *gwin;* here then we see *w* = g and oi and the Hebrew *ia* used interchangeable in the same word.

These remarks, then, will be sufficient to shew, that the principle is a universal one, and that although now and then much may seem to be built upon a similarity of words and names, yet there are real grounds to work upon.

With these introductory and preparatory remarks then we will proceed with the names of the heads of families as they are given by Biblical Authority. In the tenth chapter of Genesis we read thus, „The sons of Japheth,

1. Gomer, and Magog and Madai and Javan, and Tubal and Meshech and Tiras.

2. The sons of Gomer, or the grandsons of Japheth, Ashkenaz, and Riphath and Togarmah.

3. The sons of Javan, also the grandsons of Japheth, Elishah, Tarshish, Kittim, and Dodanim. By these were the isles of the Gentiles divided in their lands; every one after his tongue, after their families, in their nations."

The only hint given here as to the *where* we are to find these peoples is in the expression „isles of the Gentiles", and it is, therefore, important that we should understand the full meaning of the words. The Hebrew word used for *isles* is אִיִּם. But to the Hebrew mind, and in Jewish phraseology distant coastlands, and borderlands of the Gentiles represented $\kappa\alpha\tau'$ $\dot{\epsilon}\xi o\chi\dot{\eta}\nu$ those across, and on, the Mediterranean sea; so that we are naturally led to seek for Japheth and his descendants on he broad continent of Enrope, from the straits of Gibraltar westward and southward, to the Gnlph of Karskaia northward, and from the rocky Iceland to the plains of Astracan.

SECTION I.

First then as to Gomer. Homer, Orphens and Herodotus, all of them living hnndreds of years before the birth of Christ, which will carry ns back not mnch less than three thousand years, place the Kimmerians, or as we have it throngh the transposition of the Arabs, the Crimeans, in the north, that is, in the north *to them*, but more properly speaking in the countries west of the river Don, northwest of the Maiotic and the Black Sea; and the names of many places testify of their power and influence in the ahovementioned localities. According to Herodotus, the straits which nnites the Maiotic sea to the Black Sea are called after them, the βοσπορος κιμμεριος, in English the Kimmerian or Cimmerian Bosphorus; the month or outlet of the same is called κολπος κιμμεριος, the Kimmerian gulf, or bay; the isthmus which connects the peninsula of the Crimea with the continent of Russia, was called ἰσθμος κιμμερικος, now the Isthmus of Perekop, so familiar to us all; we may therefore most fairly infer that the present name of the Crimea has descended through so many hundreds of Generations and thousands of years, nothwithstanding the many vicissitudes of commerce, war, colouizations and devastations, directly and continuously from the eldest son of Japheth, namely Gomer.

The Kimmerian nation was at one period both numerous and powerful, and held the supremacy and the dominion over a great portion of the north of Europe, and, even, carried their victorious arms into the South also. According to the testimony of Herodotus, they broke into Asia Minor about the middle of seventh century before Christ, conquered the City of Sardes, and settled down along those coasts in the neighbourhood where afterwards Sinope was built. Their power and influence there, however, did not continue long; Alyattes, the father of Croesus, King of Lydia, so well known for his wealth, overcame them and drove to their native mountains and plains, where they also suffered many defeats from the then powerful and wide-spread family of the Scythians.

Since then, however, that is, since the end of the sixth century before Christ, the Greek authors make no more mention of the Kimmerians; but is it to be therefore supposed, or is it credible, that such a powerful people should vanish from the earth without leaving a vestige nor a trace behind them? Certainly not; human reason, the manners of the times, the system of continual migration, nomadic habits compel us to adopt the conclusion that, like the Kelts, the Iberians, the

Ligurians, they migrated from the East towards the West, pushed out by the more powerful and extensive race of the Scythians and Sarmatians, and that they settled down ultimately, either where they would find probably less powerful nations, or, none at all, more and more to the West and the North West. And to correspond with this hypothesis of northern migrations southward and westward, allowed to be correct by all historians, and attested by all nomadic incursions, in the course of the second century before Christ we meet with a people whose very name reminds us at once of the Kimmerians; namely the Kimberians, who at that time came in contact with the Romans, and who first filled Rome with the foreboding presentiment, that danger threatened the empire from the North.

In the meantime we find that Pliny, Pomponius Mela, Ptolemaeus testify that the Kimbrians were a people who inhabited the peninsula of Jutland, which received from them the name of Chersonesus Kimbrica; but they spread themselves from thence still further towards the West; and so we find that Strabo places the Kimbrians between the Elbe and the Rhine, Pliny coincides with him, and Cesar and Dio-Kassins reckon the Aduatici, a people inhabiting Belgium, or a part of it, among the Kimbric race. From this, then, it is clear, that this stock or particular race possessed a considerable portion of northern Germany down to the mouths and across, of the Rhine, and Holstein, Schleswig, Friesland, parts of Holland, and Belgium. From

Belgium the Cimbrians and Kymry passed over probably the straits of Dover to Lloegr or Britain, which. if we may fonnd a conjecture on the Welsh name of England, viz. Lloegr and Lloegria, might have been inhabited by a branch of the Ligurian family, bnt which must have been entirely snbdued by the Kymbrians, as the names of places first latinized and now anglicised bear abundant evidence of their victorions arms and long sojonrn, snch as York, Latin Eboracnm, Welsh or Kimmerian Efrog, or Evrog; Penrith, Welsh Penrhydd, allnding probably to the read sandstone strata; Cornwall, Kerniaw; Severn, Haveren; Thames, Thamwys; bnt they again were conqnered in their turn, and split into three sections, one portion driven to the verge of the Atlantic Ocean in Cornwall, another portion driven to the mountainons parts of Cnmberland, or *Kymry-llain*, that is, the portion of the Kymry, both of which have lost their original language, and have been swallowed np into the English nation; and a third part driven to the mountain fastnesses and recesses of Wales; and the name by which they distingnish themselves in their own language, *Kymry*, the nation, and *Kymru*, the territory of the principality, and the language, *Kymraeg*, are convincing because living proofs of a Kimmerian immigration. The language is not as some German authors suppose it to be, a mixture of German and Gallic elements, bnt the original langnage spoken by their forefathers from time immemorial, intermixed naturally with many Latin words, or, as the Kymry themselves strennously and not without the best of arguments, viz. consanguinity in origin maintain, words emanating from the same parent stock, and possessed by them independent of the Roman occupation of the island of Britain.

Now that the Kimbern of the second century before Christ were one and the same people as the Kimmerians of the seventh century, we are assnred by Plutarch, Diodorus Siculus, and the splendid geographer Strabo; and other anthors testify indirectly to the same fact. We must not snppose that when the different masses of the Kymry left their native home on the Don, that all emigrated, but according to the natural course of things, it is probable if not certain, that same portions or sections of the large and nnmerous family remained behind in different tracts of land, and submitted to the dominion and the power of the Scythians as the .Cornwallites and the Cumbrians did to the Saxons. And so we find that the first home of the Kimmerians, or the countries bordering on the Don were, towards the end of the second century before Christ the recruiting-place from whence the renowned King Mithridates, of Pontus, obtained his best soldiers, in the terrible and long struggle he had with Rome; and Justin tells us, that among them, the warriors who served in the pontish hosts, there were also Kimbrians, the remnants which I suggested that had stayed behind of the Kimmerians, and a proof, moreover, that the words *Kimmerians* and *Kimbrians* were regarded as two differently sounding names of one and the same people. In addition to this, Josephus says, that the inhabitants of Galatia were called Gomerites; but if they were, they were only a small remnant, or were so called in very ancient times; so that there is here no foundation whatever to identify or mix the great body of the Kimmerians with the Galats, or the Kelts, which some maintain are the same name, and which Aristotle uses for the Kelts of Gaul. Of the same nature also is the evidence of Pliny and Pomponius Mela, regarding the towns of Comara and the tribe Comari; if they had anything to do with the ancient Kimmerians they were the resting place of the salvage of the nation, or towns which retained their ancient names.

We have thus, then, clearly traced the Kimmerians from the greyest antiquity from their Caucasian home to their last resting place on the Welsh Hills, and have seen, also, that vast bodies of them settled down in Europe, viz. Germany, parts of Denmark, Belgium, Schleswig, Holstein and England, among the Scythians and also along the Borders of the Black Sea; such has been the fate of the children of the first-born of Japheth according to the united testimony of heathen Authors, the traces of language, the names of places, and the law of early migrations; and it is not opposed, but con- firmed, by the testimony of the Sacred Historian who has placed them, as well as the other sons of Gomer, in the isles, that is in the Coast-lands of the north and the west.

SECTION II.

The next of the sons of Japheth is Magog. All ancient authors are agreed npon this fact, that the Magogites and the Scythians ware one and the same people, that their primitive home was on the east and nordeast of the Black sea, extending from beyond, westward of the Hyperborean mountains, eastward beyond the Caspian and the Aral sea, over Siberia, and to the very confines of the Chinese empire, nnd generally designated in ancient Atlasses, Scythia intra Imaum, and Scythia extra Imanm, so called from Imans, a range of mountains, probably the Himavat (Mustag). And we have an incidental proof from Pliny, Ptolemy and Josephus, that the name Magog was a highly honorable and popnlar name among the Scythians.|

The next question, then, that remains to be decided is, who are the present representatives and descendants of the Magogites, or the Scythians. We must arrive at an answer to this question from negative inferences; we know certainly, as far as anything historical can be known, that the other countries of Enrope have been peopled by other certain families, which will be more fully proved in the course of the essay; we know that Spain was first peopled by the Iberians and Ligurians; France and Italy by the Kelts; parts of Germany and Anstria by the same and so on, and therefore we come to the conclusion, that if the Scythians were not entirely swallowed up by an almost nniversal earthquake, or by unheard-of wars, their descendants can be no other than the inhabitants of the present widely-extented empire of the Russians.

But to trace out the subject more fully. If we go eastward and northward from the habitations of the Asens or Askenians, the great German branch of the Japhetic race which we shall hereafter more fully explain, and which had settled in Almania at least eight hundred, if not more than a thousand years, before Christ, we find that from time immemorial the Scythians had been inhabiting those vast regions and dreary steppes. The name Scythian, in which, let us remember, the *c* should be properly pronounced hard, most probably signifies *Shooters,* bow-shooters, and corresponds remarkably with the indo - germanic or indo - european word *skiutau*, to shoot; we have the same traces in the German *Schütze*, English *shoot,* shooter, and the Welsh *saethu*. Diodorus Siculns informs us that then was a Scythian tradition, according to which, they lived originally on the shores of the Araxes, that is, the Wolga, and that they afterwards subdned the conntry between the Cancasian range, the Maiotic Sea and the Don. Afterwards they conquered the principalities of the Don down away into Thracia, and pushed out, as we have before hinted, the Kimmerians towards the West. According to the testimony of Herodotns, their history commenced about 1500 years before Christ; and Hesiod was in his time already acqnainted with them as a northern nation; even the egyptian hero - warrior Sesostris had to struggle with them. Thucidides says, no nation in Asia nor Europe is equal in power and in number to the Scythians, and no one could stand or resist their bravery and might, if they clung to one another. From this expression of Thucydides then, it is clearly implied, that they were separated into different stems, or tribes, or clans, and which indeed other anthors most distinctly affirm. The multiplicity of these races formed a variagated mixture, and other intermixtures produced again other inferior tribes or clans. At the commencement of the second century B. C. we meet for instance with the Roxolani, that is the Ross, or Russ-alani, an intermixture, as their name indicates, of the Ross and the Alans; in the same way we meet with Tauroscythians and Alanoscythians, Keltoskythians, and as the most powerful and most numerous of the Scythian race, we meet with the Sarmatians, who were well known as early as the time of Herodotus. As it happened with the great Germanic nation, that the name of a small tribe was ascribed to, and adopted by, the whole midland population of Europe from the green hills of Tyrole to the wawes of the Baltic, and from the turbid wawes of the zyder zee to the foot of the Carpathian Mountains, so it happened with the Scythians, that this branch of the family called Sarmatians, becoming the most important and powerful by the triumph of their arms, swallowed up gradually the ancient Scythic name, so that in the time of Pliny they were generally known under that comparatively new appellation. The Scythians had

their own peculiar language, different from other primitive races, as well as several peculiar and extensive
dialects; and so Herodotus observes that, the Sarmatians spoke Scythian, but not quite pure; and Lucian
tells us the same thing regarding the Alani, and therefore we may fairly infer that Roxolani, or the Russ-
alani, from whatever quarter the former came, had at least
one half of the Scythic element in their language. Let
us revert then to the question already proposed; in
what relationship do the Scythians stand to the modern
nations of our day? — Since we know from the historical evidences quoted above, that in ancient times
they were a mighty and populous nation, since further
there is not the slightest hint that they were extirpated
from the length and breadth of the land by any extra-
ordinary misfortune, there must be descendants of the
Scythians the same as of almost all the other great
nations of antiquity. Now we know the ancestors of
the various nations who now inhabit the western parts
of Europe, even to the banks of the Oder, namely the
Ligurians, Iberians, and the Goths of Spani, the Kelts
and Cymry of Great Britain, the Kelts, Ligurians, Goths
and Franks of Gaul, the Allemani of Germany; and
consequently we can come to no other conclusion than
that the Scythians were the progenitors of those nations
who even this very day dwell in the ancient home of
the Scythians, namely the Russians and Poles. In other
words, the Scythians were Sclaves, and their language
the Slavonic. The most irrefragable proofs testify to

the truth of this proposition; and especially that latent but visible similarity in the customs and habits of the Scythians on the one hand, and the Russians and Poles on the other hand. The literature of Germany has of late years been much enriched by the fertile pen of the accomplished and far-and-wide-traveller Kohl, and amongst other things he gives a description of the present state of things in the South of Russia, and every one who compares his description with that which Herodotus sketched some twenty three hundred years ago, must confess, that it is one and the same people that both travellers are describing. But in addition to this, we have the testimony of ancient Geographers. I have quoted above the testimony of Pliny, according to which about the commencement of the first century the name Scythians passed over into that of Sarmatians; now, Ptolemaeus says, „in Sarmatia the following principal peoples dwelt, the Wendi on the banks of the whole wendian Sea havens; upon the coasts of the Maiotic Sea dwell the Jazygen and the Roxalani, and so on;" now *Wendi* is acknowledged and well known to he the oldest proper name of the Slavonic races, a name which has been preserved to this very day. According to the statement of Ptolemaeus, the Wendi are therefore the head-people of the Scythians and Sarmatians, and consequently the Scythians or Sarmatians are the same as the Wendi, that is, they were Slaves. In addition to this, almost all Scythian words which are mentioned by ancient historians, are easily explained and deciphered either out of and by the Slavonic language itself, or from the indo-european language which is the common mother of the Slavonic, Keltic, German, Roman, and Greek languages *).

SECTION III.

We pass on now to the third son of Japheth, viz. Madai. They are the Medes: and scarcely anything more need be added where all agree. According, however, to the lately deciphered ancient persic cuneiform characters, the Medes were called Mada, and by the Semitic nations Madai, the same precisely as we have it in the Bible, an undesigned coincidence of no mean importance and interest.

According to Herodotus we find that the Medes were distinguished in antiquity by the name Arii. This name, however, comprises not only the Medes in particular, but also the most ancient Zend races, as well as the Sanscrit Indians, three original families whose near relationship can be proved by a fact which admits of no doubt, namely through the similarity of their language. It only needs to be added that in this instance we have travelled into Asia, but it requires no apology, as we have only followed the track prescribed by the Mosaic table, and have not dwelt long upon our foreign excursion.

*) See Professor Grimm, „Geschichte der deutschen Sprache".

SECTION IV.

The fourth Son of Japheth is Javan. Javan is in the whole the same or Jaon, hence *Jonia*. In the third chapter of Joel and the sixth verse it is translated Grecians in our version, the translators following tho Septuagint, who have rendered it, *υἱες Ἑλλήνων*, that is, sons of the Greeks. In Sanscrit the Greeks were called Jawana; in old Persian Juna, in the Egyptian language Junan; from these philological correspondencies alone then, it is quite clear that words from the root Javan, or *Jawan*, were names used by different nations to signify the Greeks, and that they were the descendants of the Scripture Javan. But in ancient Greece, there were four different branches of the Hellenic family, known as such above a thousand years before the christian Era; viz. the Aeoliaus, the Joniaus, the Achaians and the Dorians; but the original and most ancient head-families are allowed to be the Aolians and the' Jonians; the Dorians and the Achaians were the descendants of Aeolus; and it is now allowed by the most accomplished Greek scholar of modern times, that is Odfrey Müller, that thè Doric dialect is only a degenerate and corrupt from of the Aeolic. Now according to the testimony of Josephus, it is expressly affirmed, that the descendants of Elisha peopled that country known as the home of the Aeolians; and it is no violent transposition to trace in the word Aeolus, vestiges of the ancient name pronounced by the Hebrews *Elisa*, and it is generally allowed that Ezekiel, speaking of the „isles of Elisha", in the 27 c. 7 v. meant the islands of the Archipelago. In the word Hellas, the general name of the Greeks, we clearly find traces of Elis or Elisha, — plainer still in the name of the province Elis, in Peloponesus, in the city Elensis in Attica, and the river Elissus, in the same part of the country, and Eleus, a king of Elis. Thns then wo find the descendants of the father, Javon, or Joanians, and Elisha, the son, in the same localities. There were, indeed, in the same localities people snpposed to be still more ancient than either of these; namely the Leleges and the Pelasgi; Herodotus says that they were the original inhabitants of all those countries which go nnder the general name of Greece; bnt he says in the next paragraph, that he did not know what language they spoke; bnt so little is actually known of the Pelasgi, and what is written about them is tinged so mnch with the mythical, that it is much safer to infer, that they were no long and abiding dwellers in the land; but where they came from and who they were mnst remain an entire mystery.

Gfrörer builds a most curions theory on what Herodotus and Aristotle say; but there are two decided objections to, the one is, it implies that the deluge was not universal bnt local; and secondly, that the Leleges and the Pelasgi were actually antedelnvians who in some way or other escaped the flood, and that the Jonians and Eolians sprang from them; but if what he says could be correct, then the Jonians had nothing to do with Javan, and thns he defeats his own pnrpose.

What he says, literally translated is this, „Thus „the most ancient people of Greeco are the Aeolians and „the Jonians. But Herodotus declares both to be the „descendants of the Pelasgi. I will remark in the next „place that already among the ancient Greeks there „was a statement that the orientals wonld, instead of „Jonians, have said Jaones. In fact, the Persians, „which are introduced speaking in the well-known play „of Aeschylus, call the greek people, Jaones. A root „which appears to have sounded like Javan or Jawan, „lies at the bottom. In Sanscrit the Greeks were called „Jawana, in old Persian Jnna, in Egyptian Junan, in „Hebrew Javan. Whence may the word be derived? „Most probably from the Sanscrit Jnwan, Zend Javan, „that is *juvenis*, yonng. The Jonians then were the „yonng ones, and mnst have been so called in contra-„distinction to the old ones. Aristotle actually tells ns „that the Grecians were in remote antiquity called „γράικοι, that is, the old ones. Between the old ones, „the Graikoi, or the Pelasgi, and the Jonians, or the „young ones, some event mnst have occurred which „appeared to mankind as a renewing of the earth, or „of the human race, that is, according to all probability „that great delnge, of which, independent of the first „book of Moses, the strata of the mountains testify, „and which was well known to the Greeks under the „name of the flood of Deucalion."

But to such a theory as this, founded simply upon the supposition that the word Javan *may* have come from the Sanscrit, and that an event *may* have happened of such and such a character, some such further objections as these must inevitably suggest themselves; if the Pelasgi were an antedeluvian people, they were drowned, or they were not drowned; if they were not drowned, then the Jonians may have descended from them, and therefore had nothing whatever to do with Javan; if they *were* drowned, then they had no connection with the Jonians: in other words, it is impossible to connect the Greeks both with the antedeluvian Pelasgi and the post-deluvian Javan. According to all ancient authority then, we are assured, as far as anything historical can be assured, that Javan was the father of the Jonians, and that his descendants and the descendants of his son are to be found in the land of Greece.

SECTION V.

The next sons of Japheth are Tubal and Meshesh. These two are invariably mentioned together, and that has caused no little difficulty in satisfactorily and clearly fixing their habitation or habitations, and that of their descendants.

The testimony of Josephus says „Thobel, that is Thubal, founded the Thobelites, who are now called Iheres; and the Mosocheni were founded by Mosoch, that is Meshech." We see that by this testimony, the Tibareni of Herodotus, and the Iberes of Josephus are

the same people; that is, the descendants of Tubal,
originally inhabiting Asia Minor. But the question now
is, whither did they further migrate? Let us, however,
first clear up the word Tubal and Tibar or Tibar, or
Tybar, and Iber. It is by no means an unusual thing
for L and R to be interchanged in almost all languages.
Thus consanguineous with the Greek λείριον we have
the Latin *lilium*, a lilly; the Hebrew word שַׁרְשְׁרָה
(chain) is in the cognate dialects of the Chaldee שַׁלְשְׁלָה
Arabic سلسلة; the words אַרְמְנוֹת and אַלְמָנוֹת (palaces)
are used indifferently; so also are the words אֵלּוּ (lo)
and אֲרִי; and so again on the other hand, we see the
letter *L* hardened into *R*, as it is in Thibar or Tybar
for Tubal, in many Hebrew, Chaldee and Arabic words;

for instance, אַלְמָנָה (widow) is in Arabic أرملة חֲלָצַיִם
(loins), is in Chaldee חַרְצָא; — with these abundant
instances, then, of the interchange of the two letters,
there is nothing violent, fanciful, nor unnatural in
identifying Thubal and Thubar. Again with regard
to the prefix *T*. Moses pronounced and wrote the word
as it was familiar to him by tradition, probably as it
was familiar to the Egyptian Savans, in whose schools
he was taught; and the word was no doubt pronounced
differently by different nations; just in the same way as
the following words were variously written and pronounced by different authors, Ιαερη and Αερη, Θουρροι and
Ουρσοι, Taxyren and Axyren, Τορεται and Ορεται, Ιουρ-
κοι and Τουρκοι, Tanaitis and Anaitis.

Now we return to the question, whither did these Tibarian, or Iberians, the great bnlk of the descendents of Tnbal, of which those Thobelites and Moscheni inhabiting Armenia and the shores along the Caspian and the Black sea were but an insignificant remnant, whither did they migrate and spread themselves?

Isaiah, in the 66 chapter of his prophecies, places Tubal in connection with Javan, and both in the „isles afaroff," i. e., the inhabitants of the far west; and Josephus, as well as St. Jerome, clearly and decidedly allnde to the Iberians of Spain as Thubalites; and so, precisely to correspond with this, we know for a most positive fact, that the most ancient inhabitants of Spain, viz. the Ligurians and Iberians immigrated thither from the land of the Caucasus or Armenia in the widest signification of the word, to their second abiding place in the pyrenean peninsula. In addition to this, Phoenicians, Greeks and Romans, all agree in deriving the original inhabitants of Spain from Armenia.

The language of the old Iberians of Spain has been preserved until this present day among the people of the Basque provinces; and we meet in various parts of Spain with names of places, streams, tribes, etc., corresponding so remarkably with names of places in Armenia and the vicinities of the Black and Caspian seas, that, independent of actual tradition to the same effect, we wonld natnrally be compelled to conclnde, either that the Iberians (old Spaniards), came from Armenia, or that the Armenians from Iberia. The river Ebro,

Iberus was so denominated by the Iberians. A province of Armenia, east of the Black Sea, west from Colchis and the Caspian Sea, was called, in ancient times, Iberia, after the Iherians who dwelt there; and we know also from Pliny, that in Armenia there was a river called Iberus, like that of Spain. To the west of the Armenian Iberians, dwelt the Behryces; me meet with the same Behryces in Spain; the Chalybes, so well-known in connection with the retreat of the ten thousand, were neighbours of the Armenian Iberians; Spain had also its Chalyhes; Luhaners are a side-branch of the spanish Iberians; we meet with Lnbieners on the borders of the Armenian Iberians. Since, however, we know, that migrations were from the east westward, and never from the West eastward, we are inevitahly compelled to conclude that the Iberians came from Armenia; and so said tradition even as early as the time of Varro, who declares the Iberians to be the very oldest immigrants to Spain; Appian says they came thither from Asia; and Sallust, the well-known Roman Historian, says in his history of the Jugurthinian war, that, „translators have read to me the following acconnt ont of Phenician books which were ascribed to King Hiempsal, that in ancient times, the Armenians, who lived in Spain, had passed over from thence, and had possessed a part of Africa." Half doubtfully does he indeed impart this information out of the phoenician anthority; but as it was with Herodotns, who told many a tale which he him-self did not believe, and shook his head at their incredibility, so it was with Sallust; many discoveries made many hundreds of years after their time, have fully confirmed what they doubtoully communicated; Sallust did not know, that the ancient inhabitants of Spain, i. e., the Iberians had come from Asia, that is from Armenia; and the Phoenician books of Hiempsal were perfectly right.

Lastly, these Iberians, in the course of time, spread themselves to the South of France, to parts of the islands of the Mediterranean sea, the Balearii, Corsica, Sardinia, Sicily and even streaks of Italy, even as far as the River Tibar; these, in fact, with their neighbours the Ligurians, were so well known as an extensive and numerous people, that Hesiod called the West of Europe Ligyan or Ligurian. Thus, then, we find the descendants of Meshech and Tubal extending over vast tracts of Europe, and also a considerable remnant remaining behind in their wild, primitive and stormy home. It is erroneous to suppose, that the descendants of Meshech and Tubal expanded to the North, into Russia, Poland, or had any thing more to do with the inhabitants of those parts than a common origin, but no after intermixture in their widely separated settlementes: we have clearly shown that those vast tracts were peopled by the descendants of Magog, the Scythians and Sarmatians; and we have no historical evidence to connect Meshech and Tubal with *Moscow*, as some do, and thereby with Russia.

SECTION VI.

We now come to the last of the Sons of Japheth, *Tiras*. They are, according to Josephus, Jerome, Jonathan, and Jargum of Jerusalem, „the Thracians." But Herodotus says that the Getae were a branch of the Thracians; Strabo agrees with him in the same thing; and to place the fact beyond all doubt, he says in another place, that the Getae and the Thracians had one and the same language. Bnt Herodotns, by saying that the Getae were a branch of the Thracians could mean no more than that they were a co-branch with them; that is, that they descended from the same common stock. One nation, one family was as old as the other; and if Moses did at all refer to the Thracians under the word Thiras, (and if he did not we have no other trace of his descendants) he recognized in them an independent nation; for we must remember that the mosaic table of generations was a post facta one, and not prophetical; he spoke as he fonnd them *then*, although it has apparently the tone of an á priori demonstration of the popnlation of the earth; yet in reality Moses traces from the stream to the fountain, and not as is the vulgar and general impression, from the fonntain to the stream. We mnst be content, then, to accept those ancient authorities above qnoted, or to lose altogether the traces of Tiras descendants. We do, indeed, know enongh of the Thracians to prove that they were a mighty and an ancient nation; Herodotus says, „that after the Indians, the Thracians were the greatest people in the world. In want of unity lay their weakness."

Gfrörer, however, tries hard in some way, to identify the Thracians the Ascanians and the Germans; but many of the arguments which he uses, will apply to identify any two most distant nations of antiquity; he is correct, of course, in maintaining that they were of the same family; but he might have spared himself that trouble, for Moses had done it before him. But more of this hereafter. We have no motive now for inquiring into the habits and customs of the Thracians; otherwise, abundance of materials might be found; we merely seek in the „isles of the Gentiles," whither Moses has directed us, for the descendants of the sons of Thiras, and if the evidence adduced is not sufficiently convincing to find them in the Thracians, we have no where else to turn our eyes, and there is no other authority, ancient nor modern, that gives the slightest clue as to the fate of the youngest son of Japhet. I make these remarks principally because I know that there is another etymology given to the Thracians, which, although of a pure mythical character, might be deemed of importance by some.

PART THE SECOND.

We have hitherto, at somewhat of a disadvantage and difficulty, traced the children of Japheth, their fortune and their families, as they occur in the Mosaic genealogical Table; but as that place seems to be the best for presenting the subject in the clearest possible way to the mind's eye, we shall continue, notwithstanding the difficulties which it presents, to follow in the same course.

SECTION I.

As Gomer was the eldest son of Japheth, so was Ashkenas the eldest son of Gomer.

It would, perhaps, not be too much to say that we have traces, or remnants, of this same family in that country which was perhaps their first resting-place; in Troas in Myssia we find a river called Ascanins, a province called Ascania, a group of islands in the Aegean called the Ascanians, a lake called Ascanins, another lake called Ascania, all almost in the same immediate country lying along the Propontis. Now these places, we know, were so called as early as twelve hundred years before Christ. Homer says in the Ilias, that Phrygias out of Askania came to help the Trojans. This much, then, is clear, that the Ashkenians were for some time, at least, and a considerable branch of them for long time, the possessors of the countries along the Hellespont. But corresponding to this name, we meet with another family of people who went through the portals of the Caucasus, passed the Don, travelled northward and settled in Scandinavia. The name of these people was Askans or Asans; this is confirmed by the most ancient traditions of the northern Germans,

which have preserved, not only the remnants of the
word Ashken, bnt also the further information, that
their forefathers under that name crossed the Don from
the far East, and wandered towards the West. On the
spot of transition which this tradition makes mention of,
that is, on the Don, the greek geographer Ptolemaeus,
mentions a people called Asaei, or Asain; on the same
spot Strabo introdnces a people called ασβουργιατοι; and
to this very day there dwells in the Cancasus a people
called hy the Russian Anthors, Jasen, whom european
Travellers of later times call Aasen; a people whom
Kohl says are distingnished hy blue eyes, yellow hair,
(ancient characters of the Germans) and who speak a
language cognate with the German. „Is it not, then,
highly probable, that the Asaeens of Ptolemaens, the
Ashurgians of Strabo, are a remnant left behind by
the ancient German migrations? Couple with this what
Tacitus says of a German town called Ascihurgium
(Asenburg) not far from the Rhine, and Ptolemaeus
positively calls the Riesengebirge, which are in the
centre of Germany by the name of ὄρος ἀσκιβούργιον.
These two things then are perfectly clear, that a great
portion of the ancient Germans did migrate from the
lands of the Caucasus, or from still further east, and
therefore ont of Asia, through present Russia toward
north Germany and Scandinavia; and secondly, that
they had a name which was called Asens or Askens.
Is it, then, too bold to infer, that the Askens of Germany, who came from the Causasus, were the same

family as theAskens of Asia Minor who also came from the Caucasns? If not, then, the Germans are clearly one branch of the descendants of Ashkenaz, and the Jewish definition, fonnded no doubt npon Jewish tradition from time immemorial, is perfectly right.

There is, indeed, an apparently weighty objection to this conclusion; and that is, the present name of that nation, viz., Germans. But we must remember, that scarcely any nation in the world, none properly in Europo, has preserved the name of hoary antiqnity; the admixture of races, the fortunes of war, the peculiarities and characteristics of various families and tribes in the same stam, the variety of languages, all tend continually to shift and change the names of nations. The old Kimbrian name for Germans is Allmeiniaid; in Russ and Turkish they are called Niemetz; in French, Les Allemands, in Italian Tedeschi, in Spanish they are Aleman, and in their own language never *German*, but invariably *Deutsch;* whilst those whom we call Dutch, are by the Germans called Hollaender. We have, moreover, to remember that the great and widely spread German nation, as it now is, has not kept itself to its original stam, but has been intermisced, from the earliest times, both with nations who had migrated before and after if towards the West. We have no ancient German books to form any data upon; whatever we can gather is from Latin and Greek anthorities. The first Roman who was acquainted with the ancient Thuiskians i. e., Deutsche, was Cajns Julins Caesar; he calls them Germani, which has ever since been indiscriminately used by Greek and Roman Authors, but we are assured by Tacitus, that this was by no means the universal name of the people; on the contrary, that it was a new name, and that the Gauls first gave it to a branch of the Thiuskan people on the lower Rhine, who were Tungern, and that from thence it passed over into universal currency among the Latins and Greeks.

There, then, we have another instance of a modern name supplanting a more ancient one, and yet the name continuing to be rejected and unrecognized by the nation so called by foreigners. In no German document, from earliest antiquity down to the middle ages, is the word *German* found as a primitive and native word; it is, therefore, perfectly fair to infer, that the word *German* was a foreign word, used by Romans to designate the whole prople, but incorrectly, and rejected by the people themselves. With this the celebrated Professor J. Grimm agrees; he says it is derived from the Celtic *gairm* or *garm*, which means *noise, tumult,* and that thus, those Kelts who came in contact with the Tungern gave them the name of *shouters, bawlers,* which afterwards passed over to the whole German nation; the name was, of course, taken from their manner of carrying on their warfare, the constant and every day occupation of those barbarous times; and we have instances of the same method of ascribing names to people from similar causes, in different countries of the world. But, whether Grimm be correct or not in his etymology, the other observations and inferences rest upon clear and undeniable historical authority.

In conclusion then, while we agree with those who place a great portion of the Children of Ashkenas on the borders of the Hellespont, we infer from ancient history, equally authentic, that another portion of the same family migrated westward, and form a great part of the German nations.

SECTION II.

As to Riphat, we are informed by the writings of Josephus that Paphlagonia was originally called Rephataea; namely, the country of the Rephathites; that there was a people called Rhiphaei, and a river in the same direction or locality; that is about all we can find concerning the descendants of Riphate in *that* direction. That Josephus was partly right, is very possible, in fact very likely; that is, a part of the Riphathites migrated to Asia; but it is ·preposterous to suppose, that the great bulk of these numerous Japhetic races settled down exclusively in the narrow tract like Natolia; and so we are driven by necessity, by the nature of things, by the dearth of historical information, by the population of other countries, to turn in another direction, and seek the mass of the Rephatites elsewhere; and we must naturally follow the mighty stream of migration that rolled ever and anon to other and westward lands through the portals of the Caucasus. While allowing, then, that a portion of the Rephathites came down to Paphlagonia, we are bound to follow and find the nation in another part of the World; that is, in Europe, not to say anything about its being scriptural, for their homes in the times of Moses were אִיֵּי הַגּוֹיִם, the borderlands, coasts of the Gentiles, and not Asia Minor.

The first and most ancient tradition or information that we find as to the primitive home of the Kelts, is in the Life of Furius Camillus. Plutarch says of the Kelts, „they were said to have left their country, which was too small to maintain their vast numbers, to go in search of another. These emigrants consisted of many thousands of young and able warriors, with a still greater number of woman and children. Part of them took their route towards the northern ocean; crossed the *Rhiphaean mountains* and settled in the extreme parts of Europe;" this migration must be referred so far back at a thousand years before Christ; their first intercourse with Rome began in the fourth century before Christ.

Here then are the remnants of the most anciently known tradition as to the primitive home of the Kelts, and that is, the other side of the *Riphaean* Mountains. These Rhyphaean mountains, although they at once lead us more powerfully to the etymological fountain-head Rhiphat, or Riphath, than the Rhehaei of Stephanus in Cappadocia, are at first difficult to decide as to their precise locality.

Some say, they are the same as the Ural mountains,

which separate Asia from Europe. Others say, they are
mountains of the Interior of Russia. Others maintain
they were the Carpathians, and others again the Alps.
Lempresse says naïvely, „these mountains seem to have
existed only in the imagination of the poets; though
some make the Tanais rise there;" but he forgets that
historians and geographers speak of the Rhiphaean
mountains, as well as poets. Dionysius doubtlessly
means the Karpathians, when he says that a river
originated in the Rhiphaean mountains, which flowed
through Bernsteinland (old Prussia) towards the north
Sea; that was the Weichsel, or Vistula, which rises in
the Carpathians, and disembogues itself into the Baltic
at Dantzig. According to all probability Plutarch means
the same; but still the Riphaean mountains do seem to
be, according to the apparently contradictory testimonies
of the ancients, sort of wandering mountains; migrating,
nevertheless, from the first seat of the human family
continually towards the West, with the continually ad-
vancing, rolling tide of human billows to their permanent
resting · place. But still, however contradictory and
incredible it may sound, when properly understood this
migration of the Rhyphaean mountains westward, points
out the very marrow and sinews of the truth. The
Riphaean mountains were the home of the Kelts, their
boundary line, their horizon; that we have already seen
from Plutarch; as these latter migrated westward and
northward, from their original home, the Riphaeans are
also transferred westward and northward with them;

that is, wherever they made a long sojonrn, and left remnants and traces behind them, those mountains acquired, probably by themselves first, and then hy foreigners, the name of Riphaean mountains: in fact, the word Alps (which is only a derivation of *albus*, the snowy-crested, (compare Mont *Blanc*) are used in a not very dissimilar manner hy us now, a sort of generic name.

Before the Kelts, then arrived as far as Gaul, they dwelt in the vast regions of present Russia, in those neighbourhoods which are the frontiers of Asia and Europe. This important information rests not only on the testimony of Plutarch, but another fact testifies to its correctness.

Strabo says in the first book of his Geography, „before the more distant parts of Europe were accurately known to the Greeks, authors believed, that there were only Kelts and Iberians in the West, and only Skythians in the North and South; and it is only come to light after careful inquiry, that there were not only Iberians and Kelts in the West, but also Keltiberians; and that in the North not only Skythians, bnt also Keltoskythians." Thus, as the Keltiberians were a mixture of the Kelts and Iherians, so were the Keltoskythians a mixture of the Kelts heyond the Riphaean mountains, and the Skythians, i. e., the Magogites. We must, therefore clearly, consider it fairly proved, that the Kelts migrated from present Russia to their later more genial homes in Sonth Germany, Gaul, Britain and so on. Now from whence did they come to Russia? Clearly not from further north; that were almost impossible; not from the West; streams of emigration are never known to have proceeded from thence; as clearly they could not come from the South; such a thing is contrary to nature, viz. to migrate from the genial south to the cold north; there remains, then, no other place whence they could have come but from the East; that East was the base-lands of Ararat, and their father was Riphat, whence the name of their ancient mountain home, Riphaea; the Kelts were Riphaeans; and with this corresponds the tradition which has been preserved among the Jews from time immemorial, that Riphat was the father of that ancient mountain-people who dwelt on the riphaei montes, that is, the Kelts. What became of the Kelts of Britain is more of a national or local than a universal question, and we must dismiss this part of the essay by remarking, that it admits of very great doubt whether those who are now called Kelts, are Kelts at all; that the Welsh are not, has been clearly shewn, and strong proofs are at hand to shew, that in the Irish people there is a large admixture, if not an overwhelming praeponderance, of Iberian elements.

SECTION III.

As to *Togarmah*, Moses Chorenensis, who was himself an Armenian, mentions Thorgom as the father of their race; and other Greek authors agree with him therein, so that if we have not an abundance of evidence upon this point, still we have the recorded belief and tradition of the nation itself, that they are the descendants of Togarma. The Phrygians and Cappadocians their neighbonrs, were of the same origin. Herodotus distinctly affirms this, and says that they, therefore, wore the same accoutrements, and were marshalled under the same leaders in the Persian Hosts. Later greek anthors confirm this testimony; inasmnch as they declare that the Armenian language bore a very great resemblance to the Phrygian language; hut the country of the Thorgoms or Armenia extended from the river Enphrates on the West, to the Hyrcanian or Caspian Sea·on the East, and from the confines of Iberia in the north, to the hanks of the Tigris in the South. How, when, or hy what means the ancient name was so entirely supplanted as to leave scarcely any traces, except tradition, behind, we have not the means of ascertaining; we know that the word אֲרָם (Aram) which is probably the root of Armenia, was used in a most extensive signification and application.

SECTION IV.

THE SON OF JAVAN, ELISHA.

Whether it be more satisfactory to depend upon the similarity of names, such as Hellas, Elis Aeolus, Aeolians, Elissus, supposed to be corruptioas and remnants from *Elisha;* or to rely upon which Josephus distinctly tells us, viz., that all the Greeks came from Javan, it is allowed by all authorities and tradition that Thessaly, Boeotia, Aetolia, Attika, Acarnania, as well as the islands round about them, and the coasts of Asia minor, were first peopled and inhabited by the Aeolians. Of their transit, we know nothing; as far as we know, they may have migrated from Asia to Greece, or they may have passed over from Hellas to Asia. We know that the Karians, or Cares, had inhabited those islands long before the arrival of the Hellenes; but we do not know to what family they belonged, nor whence they came; we know, that about a thousand years before Christ they were driven from their islands, by the Hellenes, and passed over to Asia Minor; but we cannot from thence infer that the Hellenes came from Europe eastward; for in Asia Minor again they came in contact with the Greeks, and were compelled to be satisfied with the Southwest coasts, which bore their names even to the times of the Romains. After their name the islands of *Lesbos*, *Samos*, *Chios*, *Kos*, *Rhodos* etc., were called the Macarian islands; for the prefix *ma* signifies in many ancient languages, the habitation, or *home* of a people. The Jewish tradition identifies these Cares with the Kittites; but there is reason to doubt its accuracy from the discoveries and investigation of modern times, as we shall hereafter see; in the case of Elisha, however, in the absence of better evidence, as well as in the absence of contradictory evidence, we must conclude that Aeolians are the Elishaites of Scripture.

SECTION V.

TARSHISH.

As modern writers say, it is Tartessus in Spain. Josephus, on the other hand says that Cilicia was formerly called Tarshish. Both may be correct; Tartessus in Spain being but a small colony of some chief family or nation, settled there for the sake of its wealth, as the Anglo-Saxons of California and Australia; we see from every allusion to them that they were maritime people, precisely the people to found colonies, as we see the English do now. But where are we to seek for the bulk of the people? Did this branch of the Japhetic family become extinct? Were they driven from Cilicia to the sea? Did they not increase, like the other nations? It was impossible for a small tract like Asia minor to accommodate nations of their character for ever; we cannot suppose, that they were annihilated, neither is it probable that, so early as the time of Moses, at least, they were swallowed up by, or merged into, the surrounding nations, many of whom, as far as we know, were not more numerous, nor more victorious than themselves; and many of whom, as the sequel clearly shews, were not so able nor so adventurous as they. We are bound, then, to look for them somewhere, as a distinct material people, maintaining their nationality and their progressive character.

Long before the Trojan war, we read of a people who entered the Apennine Peninsula, a people whose name has come down even to the present day, and with whom the morning - dawn of Italian history first opens. These people are mentioned under different names, all of which, however, may be referred to one common root. Some call them Tuscer, Tusculer, Etruscans, others call them Tyrrhenians, Tyrsians; and others again Rasenas. Upon ancient inscriptions they are designated Tursni, Tursci and Tarsci*). It is quite clear, then, at all events as clear as any such inferences which are made from similarities with other names, for instance Elis, Hellas, and Elisha, that a root like Turs, Tirsis, or Tarsis must be at the bottom of these manifold forms. In a short time, these Tyrsians or Tarsians, or Tyrrheners, became the most powerful people of the Peninsula, and extended their dominion from central Italy, on the one side, southwards as far as the point of Apulia; on the other side, northward, as far as the green hills and vales of present Tyrol. And for this reasons it was that some later Greeks, who knew the antiquities of Italy only superficially, represented the Tyrrhenians as the lords of all Italy.

The prosperity and developement of these Tursci, must have already begun before the Trojan War, that is, before the year twelve hundred before Christ; for the testimony of Livy, that they had already acquired a great power about the time already stated, is deserving of all credit. What immediate country, then, did

---

*) See *Gerlach*, *Bachofen* and *Knobel*.

these Tyrrhenians, who played so important a part in the
worlds history, hefore Rome's imperial course commenced, came from? *). During the last thirty years, new
and reliahle resources have heen discovered by the opening
of ancient etruscan coffins and hurial-places, which af-
ford a comparatively easy answer to the ahove question,
and which present an astonishing representation of the
social condition, of the power, the influence and the art
of the Tyrrhenians through a long period of years.
There is no doubt, that Greek manners and hahits had
a powerful influence upon the developement of the
Etruscans, but that was the case only in comparatively
latter times. The most ancient monuments of Etruria,
and especially the vaults formed in the rocks, have their
own peculiar characteristic, in their plan, design and
execution; they are not Grecian; and many of the ob-
jects which are found in them, remind one of the
egyptian style of art; the paintings which cover the
walls, the carriage of the figures, the mode and manner of the represented play, the form of the wind-in-
struments, the pomp of domestic life, the luxuriousness
of the banquets, all hreath of a horder asiatic origin.
To a similar origin the old etruscan language poinis; it
shews no traces of relationship with the Oskian, the
Umbrian nor Latin; least of all with the Greek; and
Herodotus, no doubt from personal observation, testifies
to its entire dissimilarity to the Pelasgic idiom. In ad-

*) *Gfrörer.*

dition to this comes the peculiarity of the tyrrhenian writing, which does not, like the rest of European languages, run from right to left, but, on the contrary, from left to right; in fact many customs and arrangements, the particular division of the people into families and castes, the hard feudalisme of the peasant portion of the population, the frequent recurrence and application of the numbers three and four in their religions, as well as in their political economy, the consecration of their kings, the splendour of the governing powers, the magnificent vestures of the Lucumonae, or nobility (the tunic and praetexta originate from the Etruscans), and the high importance in which the horse was held, all lead us to conclude upon a border asiatic origin. But from what part of Asia? Herodotus gives a full description of the monument of the lydian King Alyattes, a work the greatness of which can be compared only with the Egyptian monuments. On the other hand, we have, from the pen of the Roman Varro, the description of a monument which is ascribed to the Etruscan king Porsenna, the renowned antagonist of the young roman Republic; and both these descriptions correspond with one another, in a most astonishing manner; and the designs and the execution are most wonderfully alike. We cannot, however, suppose that such remarkable coincidence is merely accidental; on the contrary, the probability assumes an overwhelming conviction, that the monuments of the lydian and etruscan kings, resemble each other so much, because the Tyrrhenians were, in some way or other, connected with the Lydians of Asia Minor.

So much for conjecture and inference; — but in point of fact, all historical evidences derive the Tyrsenians of Italy from the Lydians. Herodotus *) tells us, as the native tradition of the Lydians, that a colony which had left them, and had gone to sea, had established the power and the name of Tyrshenish people. Tacitus brings forward in 4 book of the Annals, 55 chapter, an ancient record, according to which the towns of Etruria declare, that they were descended from a colony which had been led to Asia by Tyrsenus, the son of the lydian King Atyes; other roman authors declare the same thing **). In fact, unless one runs contrary to the most valid testimony of antiquity, nothing is so clear and unmistakable, as the Lydian origin of the tyrrhenian people.

Now as to their maritime power. On this point the unanimity of the ancients is most perfect. They ruled not only the Adriatic Sea, but also the western Ocean; were known as powerful pirates, and conquered the islands of Corsika and Sardinia ***). Is it likely, that with their naval knowledge and maritime experience they should remain ignorant of the gold coasts of Spain, and if not ignorant, certainly not untempted? —. The contrary was undoubtedly the case. The Etruscan tradition

*) 1 Book — 94.

**) See Gerlach and Bachofen I. 119.

***) See Knobels proof quotations.

makes mention of a hero called Tarcho, the son of Tyr-
rhenns, who is said to have built the metropolis Tar-
chonium, (in Latin Tarquinii). But in Spain there was
not only a Tarrako, bnt a whole province which was
called Tarraconensis. To the same Tarcho the building
of the etruscan town Cortona is ascribed. Very well;
we find a town of the same name in Spain; according
to the testimony of Artemidor, the Iberians of Spain,
in addition to their own writing, made use of an old-
italian writing, that is the tyrrhenian; and in point of
fact, in the South of Spain, ancient coins have been
fonnd, the inscriptions of which are undoubtedly tyrrhenian. Still more, there was in Spain a town, and
a large district, well-known on account of its silver
mines, the name of which was Tartessns, coinciding
with the etrnscan radical word; according to that then,
the Tyrsenians of Italy must have sent colonies to
Spain, a fact which will as well account for the origin
of the tarshishan Colony in Spain, as it acconnts for
the later local habitations of the descendants of Tarshish. That Tarshish in Spain is of an older origin than
a phoenician, is clear from the fact, that Tarshish was
a place known at the commencement of Syrian prosperity, and not a place created and named, as Gfrörer
seems to imply in his article on the „Phoenicians," by
the Phoenicians themselves; for the Phoenicians, in the
widest acceptation of the word, did not begin their
colonizations, nor fully develope their maritime powers,
until the Syrian power sprang np on the rnins of

Sidonian commerce; although the Sidonians themselves had, about 1500 or 1400 before Christ, Hippo in Africa, Itanos in Crete, Oliaros in the Egean Sea, as well as other places on the south coast of Laconia.

SECTION VI.

KITTIM.

The most ancient authorities can carry us no further back on the subject of Chittim, than that they inhabited the Islands of Cyprus and Crete. Gfrörer would identify the Carians, to whom we have already alluded, with the sons of Chittim; but he offers no further evidence than the Jewish tradition.

The truth with regard to this signification, is thus expressed by Josephus, Antiquities 1. Book. 6 ch. 1 p. „Kettim possessed the island of Kettima; and this is now called Cyprus; and from this island all islands and most places by the sea are by the Hebrews called Chettim. And a proof of my assertion is, that one of the powerful cities in Cyprus has preserved the name. This is called Chitios by those who render it into Greek." Also by Epiphanius, bishop of Cyprus, a native of Palestine, and acquainted with Greek learning, e. g. against Haeres. 30, 25: „it is clear to every one that the island of Cyprus is called Kittion; for the Kittims are the Cyprians and the Rhodians." Hence it appears, that some included Rhodus as well as Cyprus under this name.

From this then, as well as other testimonies we may

most safely conclude, that the posterity of Chittim took early possession of the great islands of the Mediterranean Sea and the Archipelago, and that the undefined coastlands extending beyond them, which were not known to the unmaritime Hebrews by any particular name, are also included under the same name. Whence they came thither we cannot ascertain; it is simply possible that they came from Cilicia, but we have no sufficient evidence to ground an opinion.

However satisfactory and clear all this may be, there is a positive expression in the opinion of Gesenius which it is extremely difficult, if not impossible, to reconcile with the Mosaic table. He says, that „Kittim was founded by the Phoenicians." Now we know that the Phoenicians were a Hamitic race; they were the same as the Canaanites; whereas it is distinctly stated that Chittim was the son of Japheth. Now Moses wrote about fifteen hundred years before Christ; the fame of the Kittites had, even so early, spread for into the mountains of the East, as we see from the prophecy of Balaam; but if we assign as early a date as possible to the colonization of Cyprus by the Kittites, still we can not go far beyond 2300 before Christ, for we are directly hemmed in by the Deluge; whereas, if we are to believe the testimony of the priests of Tyrus, which they gave to Herodotus, and which he confirms in another way, the metropolis of the Phenicians was built at least 2750 years before Christ; that is, about four hundred years before the deluge. I will let Herodotus speak for himself. On his great journey be visited Tyrns and gathered information respecting the antiqnity of the city. Herodotus visited this place 450 before Christ; therefore, if the evidence of the priests be correct, the bnilding of the temple and the town dates back 2750 before Christ, and conseqnently in the eleventh egyptian dynasty of Manethos. But there is no reason from profane history why the above quotation shonld not be believed; for not only is the chronology of the Phenicians generally distinguished on acconnt of its accuracy, but the number of Herodotus is confirmed by other testimonies. Philo of Byblns, who translated the Phenician book that goes under the name of Sanchuniathon, maintains that Belus, the founder of Babylon and Tyre, flourished 2000 years before the Semiramis whom Herodotus mentions. This Semiramis lived, according to his representation, five ages (hnman-lives) or five times thirty years, that is 150 years before the babylonish queen Nitokris, whom the same Herodotns places in the year 600 before Christ. By this calculation, then, the building of Tyre reaches, according to Philo of Byblus' calculation, into precisely the same point of time as that indicated by the priests of Hercnles, namely into the 2750 th year before Christ *). Since, then, the claim of the Phenicians reaches to snch great antiquity, we must snppose, either that the descendants of Chittim migrated to these localities after

*) See Movers Phenicians II, 253.

the Phenicians, and named the islands after their own name, that the inscriptions to which Gesenius alludes, are of a pre-chittemite origin and antiquity, *or*, that some unknown hordes migrated thither, and adopted the primitive name of the conntry, *or* that the inhabitants were pure Phenicians from beginning and end. One thing is quite clear, however these difficulties may be solved, that the lands and islands in question are the localities meant by the Kittim of the Holy Scriptures.

SECTION VII.

DODANIM.

Of all the sons of Japheth, Dodanim is the one who has left the least traces behind him, and exercised the least influence, that we know of, in the world. Learned men and ancient manuscripts, and old translations are not even agreed as to the proper reading of the word. The plural form of the word, shews, almost decisively, that Moses did not mean one single individual grandson of Japhet by the word, but the tribe, or people, or nation so called, whatever reading may now be adopted, which had descended from the first son of Noah, through Javan.

With regard to the rendering of the word דֹדָנִים (Dodanim), I observe

1. The Septuagint translates the word to Ῥόδιοι, that is Rhodians, that is the ד (D or Daleth) is rendered as if it were ר (Resh or R). This is contrary to Jewish tradition.

2. The Samaritan Pentateuch agrees with the above rendering, that is, it has ר (Resh, or R) and not ד (Daleth or D).

3. The textus receptus, that, namely from which our translation is made, has, in the 1 Chronicles 1, 7, *R*hodanim, and not *D*odanim, as it is rendered in our version.

4. Jerome, although no great authority upon these matters, Eusebius and Epiphanius, himself a Cyprian lean to that view, and think that the Rhodians are the people meant.

But in answer to this, not to mention how preposterous it is to suppose that a small patch of island like Rhodes, not much larger than a mans hand, should to be assigned to one of the grandsons of Japheth, whilst the others people vast territories, it must, at once, be distinctly stated, that the undoubted weight of authority is for *D*odanim and not *R*hodanim, and that Rhodes is, by no means, the place meant by the Dodanim of Scriptures. We dismiss therefore the Rhodians, as well as the Dodona of Epirus, and seek for a more satisfactory and expansive explanation elsewhere, and for a more prolific posterity to Dodanim than in a petty island, or in an obscure town, about the precise position of which learned men do not agree.

According to the authority of the Midrasch דֹּדָנִים (Dodanim) is contracted, or softened from דַּרְדָּנִים (Dardanim) and hence, probably, the confusion above alluded to between the letters D and R, in Hebrew

Manuscripts. That this softening is of frequent occurrence Gesenius refers to the Phenician Monuments to prove. This solution, then, refers us, at once, to the Dardanians, that is, not only the Trojans of Troas, but their blood-relations west of the Thracians on the Adriatic Sea in Illyria; and this agrees with Jewish tradition. The Dodanims were the Illyrians. The Illyrians became more accurately known to the civilized people of Greece only since the times of Philip of Macedon and his son Alexander, both of whom waged war with them. Since this more intimate acquaintance began, the race of the *Dardanes* becomes prominent as the most powerful of the Illyrians. Most ancient traditions not only make mention, of the Dardanes, but bring them into the very closest relationship with the Trojans of Asia Minor. According to the statement *) of Strabo, of Nicolas of Damascus, and of Appian, Dardanus, a son of Illyrius was the father of the Dardanes. This Dardanus according to Homer **), founded the Trojan Kingdom. In whatever light we look upon these somewhat perhaps distorted ancient traditions, one thing is clear, from them as well as from elsewhere, and that is, that the Dardaniens of Europe stand in the closest intimacy with a people of the same name in Asia Minor, and that, indeed, according to the tradition, it was Dardanians from Europe that founded the Trojan kingdom, and not the converse, that Trojans emigrated

*) Knobel p. 105.

**) Iliad. 20, 215 $\varkappa. \tau. \lambda.$

to the europaean Dardaniens. The juncture between
the two halves or branches was the island of Samothrace,
which according to the testimony of Pliny was once
called Dardania. The Dardanians were considered by
the most ancient Greeks as near relations; their language
had a great similarity to the Hellenic; but was, on the
contrary, totally different from the Phrygian. This explanation, then, corresponds with the Mosaic location of
אִיֵּי הַגּוֹיִם, the coastlands of the Gentiles; and we have
thus all the Sons of Javan grouped together on the
coastlands of the Mediterranean Sea, each fitting in his
own place, like sockets in mortises, without tripping
the heels or treading on the toes of their brethren.

Corrigenda.

Pag. 4 l. 17 read *llyſn*
  ,, 9 ,, 11 ,, *red* for *read*
  ,, 12 ,, 4 ,, *were* ,, *ware*
  ,, 13 ,, 17 ,, *there* ,, *then*
  ,, 14 ,, 21 ,, *waves*
  ,, 18 ,, 23 ,, *form* ,, *from*
  ,, 25 ,, 23 ,, *settlements*
  ,, 30 ,, 23 ,, *intermixed*
  ,, — ,, 25 ,, *it* for *if*